An Around-the-World Alphabet

An Around-the-World Alphabet

by Jeanne Jeffares

Peter Bedrick Books
New York

A is for angel,
apple, ancient
Athenian,
athlete, ape
and artist and
anemones.

B
is for Babylonian,
ball, bust, boat, bow, banana.

is for C
cockle shell,
crocodile,
cactus,
cherries,
conifer, cats
and carp.

D is for ding-dong bells, dunce, dromedary, dianthus.

E is for
eskimo
and Eve
(in the garden of)
Eden, elephants
and eating.

F

is for frogs,
fishing for
fishes, a
fort, figs
and for fairies.

G is for

gondola, giraffes, garland, gloves, grapes.

H is for hens,
holly,
hippopotamus, helmet, hats,
hypericum, house.

I is for invalid, identical twins, Indian rope trick, immersion, Irish moss, ink caps, ivy.

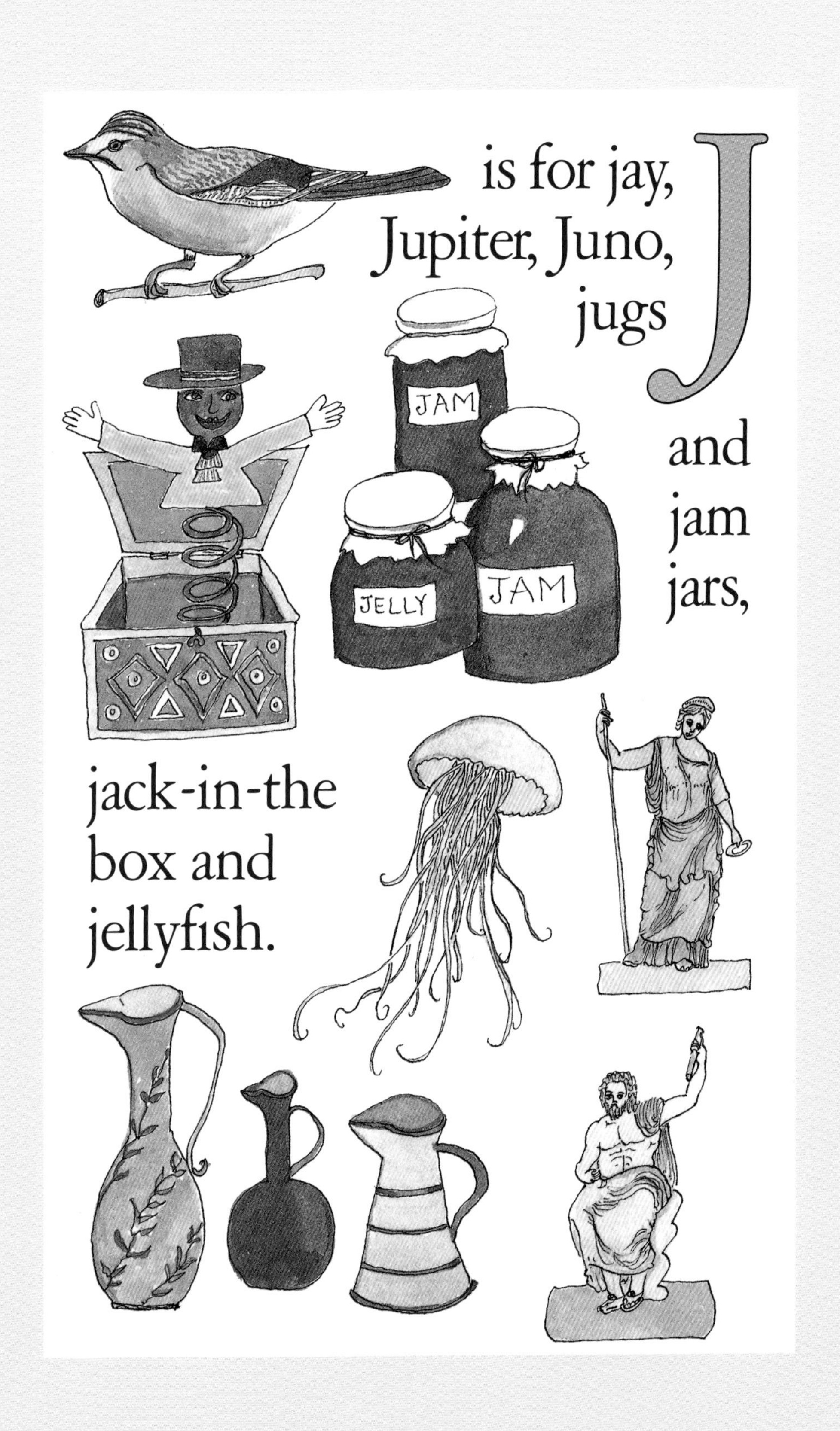

J is for jay,
Jupiter, Juno,
jugs
and
jam
jars,
jack-in-the
box and
jellyfish.

K is for kettle,
kangaroo,
kepi and
king
and kale,
kirk,
karate.

a Letter with Lots of Love from Lucy Locket.
L
L is for
lobster,
llamas,
ladder and liberty,
lemon
and a
letter.

M is for mangel-wurzel,
Madonna,
marigold,
magician,
mackerel.

is for Napoleon,
N
nautch-wali
and nasturtium,
Neptune, nest
and nautilus.

OBELISK.
O is for
Orion, ostrich,
octopus, obelisk
and olive branch.

P
is for
patchwork quilt,
pail and
panda,
pears
and
penguins
and
palm
tree.

Q is for quack and quail and queue and quill and quaking grass
and queen.
Quack
QUACK

R is for rabbits, ram
and Russian dancer,
rose, ruin, rainbow
and robin redbreast.

S is for snowman and scarf, stork,
snowdrops, shoes
and sabots,
scorpion and

sun.

T is for travellers joy (clematis vitalba), tutu, tomahawk, tonsure, teapot, tiger, tattoo

U
is for
an Ursuline nun
with an umbrella,
upside-down
urns
and
utensils.

V
is for
vehicles and viper,
viaduct, veil,
violin and
volcano.

W
is for
water lily, waistcoat,
watering can,
washing line,
watch and wattle.

X is for xmas tree.
XMAS LOVE.

Y is for
yacht,
yak and
yeoman, yashmaks,
yule log at yule tide.

and

Z

is for

zephyr, zebra, zorilla and zodiac.

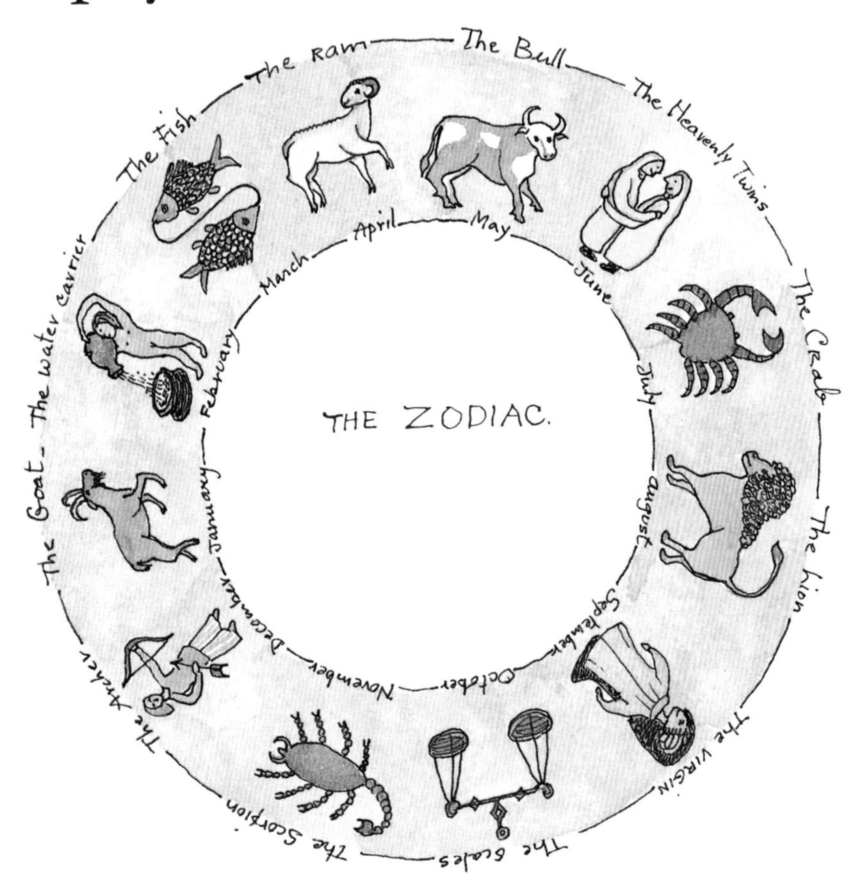

An *Around-the-World* glossary.

Anemone	A small wild flower found in woods
Babylonian	A person who came from the ancient civilisation of Babylon
Bust	A sculpture of the chest and head
Carp	A fresh-water fish
Dianthus	The plant family to which the pink in the picture belongs
Dromedary	A one-humped Arabian camel
Hypericum	The plant family to which the yellow flower in the picture belongs
Juno	The wife of the Roman god Jupiter
Jupiter	The chief god of the Romans; the god of gods
Kale	A cabbage with open curled leaves
Kepi	A cap worn by French soldiers
Kirk	A Scottish church

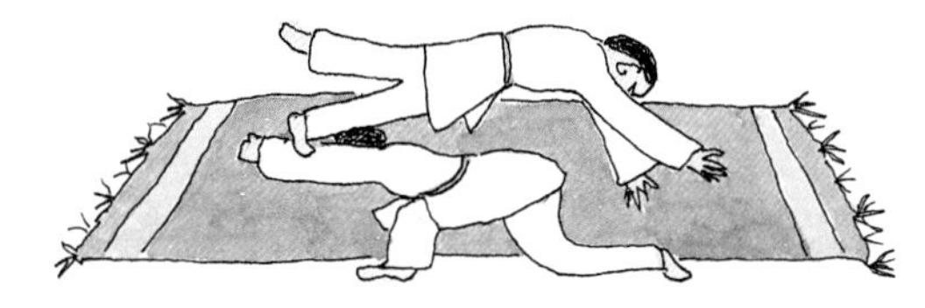

Karate	The famous art of unarmed combat from Japan
Liberty	Freedom; the statue of Liberty is in New York harbour
Llama	South American animal often used to carry things
Mangel-wurzel	A variety of beet grown for cattle
Nautilus	A shell from the Southern Seas
Neptune	Roman god of the sea

Nautch-wali	A professional dancing woman in India
Obelisk	Tall, four-sided, pointed pillar made from one stone
Orion	A constellation, or group, of seven very bright stars, three of which form Orion's belt
Quail	A type of game-bird from the partridge family
Quaking grass	A moorland grass
Sabot	A French peasant's wooden shoe
Tomahawk	A North American Indian war axe
Tonsure	The act of shaving part of the head by priests and monks
Traveller's-joy	A wild plant that grows by the roadside and is sometimes called 'old man's beard'
Tutu	A ballet dancer's short, stiff, spreading skirt
Ursuline nun	A nun who follows the teachings of Saint Ursula
Viaduct	A bridge carrying a road or railway over a valley
Viper	A type of snake
Yak	A kind of ox from Tibet
Yashmaks	A double veil worn by Muslim women, worshippers of Mohammed
Yule log	A log set alight to celebrate Christmas
Zorilla	An African skunk-like animal
Zephyr	The Greek god of the west wind

First American edition published in 1989 by
Peter Bedrick Books, New York

Published by agreement with Canongate Publishing Limited

Library of Congress Cataloging in Publication Data

Jeffares, Jeanne.
An around-the-world alphabet / by Jeanne Jeffares.
1st American ed.
p. cm.
Summary: Introduces the letters of the alphabet with illustrative words drawn from various cultures around the world.
ISBN 0-87226-324-X
1. English language—Alphabet—Juvenile literature.
[1. Alphabet.] I. Title. PE1155.J43 1989 [E]—dc 19

Designed by Tim Robertson
Printed and bound in Great Britain